RIPPLES

[stories]

ANDREW ST. JOHN

These stories are works of fiction. Names, characters, places, and incidents either are the products of the author's imagination or are used fictitiously. Any resemblance to actual persons, living or dead, businesses, companies, events, or locales is entirely coincidental.

© 2019, 2023 Andrew St. John

All rights reserved. No portion of this book may be reproduced in any form without permission from the publisher, except as permitted by U.S. copyright law.

Cover photo credits: giselaatje, simonwijers, and jclk8888. www.pixabay.com

Cover design by Andrew St. John

ISBN: 9781079734805

*For the family and friends who taught me what
unconditional love really means.*

CONTENTS

I. Secret	1
II. Hurt	19
III. Help	38
IV. Ripples	48
V. Ants	62
VI. Gone	68
VII. Shells	77

I. Secret

The two lunch waitresses at Vickie's Diner hung their aprons on the hooks just inside the kitchen, then crossed the dining room toward the door with their modest tips shoved into their jeans pockets.

"Have a nice weekend, ladies. See y'all on Monday," Vickie called as she wiped lunch-rush debris from the tables.

"Buh-bye," they chimed in unison.

The bell over the door clinked behind them, and the dining room fell silent. Save for the swishing of the industrial dishwasher in the back, the place was devoid of sound. This meant the radio, an old AM/FM boombox on a shelf above the cash

RIPPLES

register, had once again powered down of its own accord. Vickie sighed and dragged a black metal chair around the counter. Climbing atop the thick, vinyl-covered seat, she could just reach the cord protruding from behind the radio. She pulled it from the socket, then strained to reinsert it, a move that required she stand on the tips of her toes and produced a sharp ache in her thick calves.

Though she was well into her fifties, Vickie had mostly avoided the middle-aged softness that usually accompanied a long, easy marriage and a couple of children. Still, her body had lately begun protesting all the hard work she demanded of it.

As the last few notes of "Nearer, My God, to Thee" again crackled through the speakers from a local Christian/Gospel station, she heard the bell above the front door ring. She stepped with a soft thud back to the floor and, without turning around, said, "Forget something?" assuming that Tracy had once again left behind her purse or her key ring.

"Are you open?" replied a man's voice.

She turned around then, startled only slightly, and said, "Sure, come on in. Just have a seat if you can find a clean spot."

He glanced at the table beside him underneath the large plate-glass window facing the square and, seeing that it was bare of any dishes, sat down quietly. From where Vickie stood, he appeared to be in his mid-forties and more than a little handsome. He wore a striped golf shirt tucked carefully into neatly pressed khaki shorts. The vivid blue and white stripes on his shirt were so narrow and the contrast between the two colors so high that it seemed to shimmer as he moved. The loafers he wore also shone brightly.

She had never seen this man before, but Vickie felt she could guess a great deal about him. Probably he wore an expensive suit and drove a Lexus to his job as a lawyer or accountant. Even the faintly graying hair around his temples suggested a prestigious career, a gorgeous wife, and one or two accomplished teenage children.

He thumbed the plastic menu open but seemed almost not to be reading it. Vickie walked over to the table with a damp white dish towel and scooped a few crumbs from the tabletop onto the floor.

"What can I get you to drink, sweetie?" Vickie asked.

As a woman raised in the warm, red-dirt heart of Georgia and well into that matronly age beyond raising children, she freely exercised her natural right to call anyone and everyone by pet names. Most people, unless they had fallen out of her favor, were Sugar or Honey or some variation thereof.

RIPPLES

"Sweet iced tea," he replied without looking up. "Please." The last word slipped out automatically, a reflex dulled somewhat by time but still keen.

"Sure thing. You need a minute?" She stuck her fists on her hips, one still clutching the damp towel.

"Yes," he said in the same flat tone.

Most people who came into the place alone in the off hours were generally quiet, but this man's subdued demeanor was noticeably artificial. He didn't seem interested in conversation, nor did he give any sign that he wanted to be left alone, as most solitary patrons did when they had some work to do or a book to read.

"Mm-kay, I'll be right back with your tea. You need lemon?"

He did not answer her this time, so she turned and trudged back to the kitchen without any further interrogation.

On the radio, Leann Rimes twanged "Amazing Grace." She wasn't as good as Judy Collins, but the song nonetheless elicited a deep, soulful hum from Vickie's throat as she crossed the small dining room. In the back, she filled a translucent red cup with ice cubes and sweet tea, then scooped a couple of lemon slices onto a saucer, just in case. Still humming, she came back to the table and found the man sitting with the menu closed in front of him, his head turned slightly to stare out the window facing the street. He seemed to be looking at the car parked in front of the cafe, a brilliant black Volvo.

Not even close, Vickie thought.

"All set?" she asked as she set down his drink and a paper-wrapped straw.

He was silent for a moment. Then he turned his head and, for the first time, actually looked at the woman who had been speaking to him. She saw that he had blue-gray eyes, a remarkable color so icy and deep that the hairs on her neck and arms prickled. It wasn't the way he looked at her; there was no malice or threat at all. It was the impossible concrete color of his eyes, coupled with the long, straight nose and daring cheekbones, which produced the unsettling effect that he could see straight through her. In the long train of people she'd seen in her lifetime, she had never been so startled merely by someone's appearance.

"I'll have the grilled chicken sandwich, please. Hold the tomato."

His voice still conveyed no feeling, no hint of displeasure or satisfaction. It was as if it had been ironed flat. She could see now that his face was as impeccably maintained as his physique and clothing. There was not a spot of razor burn on his shorn cheeks, nor a single stray eyebrow. It occurred to her that he may actually be military; no man was that meticulous about his appearance unless he wore a uniform. Still, despite the crisp countenance, something like fatigue pooled darkly underneath his eyes.

"Right," Vickie said. "I'll get that going for you."

She was aware of an uneasy sensation spreading inside her abdomen. It started in the guts below her stomach and climbed upward toward the vitals underneath her rib cage. She was still not afraid of him, but something about him was simply off, like when the soundtrack in a movie is a fraction of a second behind the picture.

She stuck her head through the kitchen door and called out the order to Gabe, the cook (also the busboy, dishwasher, and handyman). He looked up from the pile of silverware he'd been sorting and rolling up into individual napkins.

"Yes, ma'am. Coming right up."

Vickie grabbed one of the silverware bundles and was about to leave the kitchen as the raw chicken breast hit the flat-top grill with a hiss. Stopping just behind the swinging door, she watched through the plexiglass porthole as the man pulled something from his pocket and held it in his fingertips. It was small and oblong, about the size and shape of a pecan. He slowly turned it over and over with his fingers as if inspecting it.

Secret

He set it down on the table and swiped one end of it with the tip of his finger and watched it spin. From where she stood, she could see the dark object spinning in tight circles. Each time it slowed, he tapped it again. It seemed to mesmerize him.

She left the sounds of sizzling chicken and whistling Gabe in the kitchen, crossed the tiled dining room floor, and placed the silverware down on the table in front of her singular guest. The spinning object, she now saw, was a rock—black, shiny, and smooth. He stopped it with the tip of his forefinger. Now she could see some fine streaks of white slicing lengthwise through it, almost like lightning bolts against a coal-black sky. He said nothing.

"Getcha something while you wait? Pack of crackers?"

"No, thank you," he answered.

"So, are you just passing through? I haven't seen you in here before." She wasn't always so invasive, but she couldn't quite still her curiosity.

"Yes," he replied. "Headed home."

He absently traced a line through the condensation forming on the outside of his cup. She considered asking where home was, but she checked herself.

"All right, I'll leave you be. Sandwich'll be out in a minute. Holler if you need me."

RIPPLES

She resumed her chore of busing the tables, piling dirty plates and silver into a gray tub and lugging each load to the back for Gabe to rinse, rack, and run through the dishwasher. She wiped down tables, refilled salt shakers, swept up crumbs and balled-up napkins, straightened chairs. All the while, she stole repeated glances at the lone diner seated by the front window. He never spoke. He never looked at her. He never made any noise at all. Occasionally, he'd spin the rock and watch as it slowly came to rest again. His silence wasn't merely an absence of sound—it was palpable, present in a way that she found simultaneously troubling and familiar. He moved stiffly as if under a tremendous weight.

Grief? she wondered.

When her father died five years before, she remembered feeling as though someone had torn a hole in her, revealing a gaping darkness that grew bigger and bigger until she could no longer see anything else. Not even the customary wagon train of mourning casseroles from her neighbors and church friends could pry through that opaque cloud. Now, looking at the beleaguered gentleman sitting at table six, Vickie thought she could see his suffering as clearly as she had felt her own.

When Gabe yodeled the "order up" signal, she delivered the grilled chicken sandwich, sans

Secret

tomato, to her patient customer. The *clonk* of the plate against the table freed him from his reverie, or whatever it was that had silenced him for so long.

"Thank you." He said it almost to the sandwich instead of Vickie. He made no move to pick it up at first.

"Everything look all right?" Vickie asked.

"Yes, thanks."

She took his continued silence as a tacit request to leave and returned to the business of prepping for the dinner shift. As she resumed the work, she furtively watched the man eat a couple of bites of the sandwich. At first, he chewed slowly and deliberately, tentatively even, perhaps a matter of shyness because he could feel her watching him. Soon, though, he ate as if he were starving. The sandwich disappeared first and then the french fries. He scraped up piles of ketchup with each one, and despite the sudden haste with which he finished his meal, he never dropped a single crumb.

Vickie had just reached the table adjacent to his and was in the middle of loading a handful of napkins into the dispenser when she saw him slide his plate a couple of inches away from him. He wiped his mouth and dropped the napkin on the plate, then laid the fork and spoon on top.

As she finished arranging the condiments and

sugar caddy, she asked, "How was it?"

"Very good, thank you." He paused. Then almost to himself, he said, "I didn't realize how hungry I was."

"Would you like some dessert? There's fresh coffee brewing, and I make a mean buttermilk pie," she offered with only a trace of brag.

He declined, politely.

Vickie's curiosity finally overwhelmed her manners. "Sugar, do you mind if I . . ." She paused. "I'm not usually one to pry, but—well, are you okay?"

He manufactured a brief smile and stared at her. "Oh, I'm fine," he replied.

He turned his gaze again to the outside, to something that lingered very close to him but was invisible to her.

As his silence echoed around her, the urge to apologize flooded her chest. "Look, I'm . . ." Her voice trailed away, leaving the "sorry" hanging inaudibly in the air between them.

He stared at her with those shattering blue eyes for a moment. "You know, maybe a slice of pie and some coffee would be good."

"Coming right up," she said as she scooped up his plate and scooted back to the kitchen.

A few minutes later, the pie was gone, and all that remained was a gooey smear on the plate. She offered him another, but he asked instead for the check. She pulled a small pad from the pocket of her apron and tore off the top sheet. As he reached for his wallet, Vickie could see the strain in his movements. Whatever ghost of a smile she might have witnessed was gone, melted into the flat line of melancholy again.

The wallet he retrieved from his pocket bore no resemblance to the obsessively sharp appearance that characterized nearly every other aspect of his person. It was a thin bifold, worn to the bare seams along every edge. Scratches of various length and severity crisscrossed the tea-colored leather.

"Have you ever . . ." he began.

Vickie waited a few seconds for him to finish the question, then, sensing that it was not coming on its own, slowly pulled out the chair across from him and slid into it. She leaned forward with her arms crossed on the table.

The man buried his eyes in hers and seemed to be considering his next words very carefully. "Have you ever made a choice that, as soon as you made it, you wish you could take it back? But you can't, and it ends up destroying everything around you. Like kicking a rock down a hill and watching it bounce against the other rocks until it's basically a landslide that you can't control." He punctuated the question by picking up the glossy black stone and rolling it between his thumb and forefinger.

RIPPLES

"Well, yes. I've made some mistakes before. I mean, everyone has. We—"

"I'm not talking about a mistake. A mistake is a careless accident, something you do without realizing it. No, I mean doing something that you know from the start is wrong, but you do it anyway. You do it because you don't care about the consequences. You do it because, deep down, it's what you really want."

When he stopped, she looked at him, searching carefully the lines that creased beside his eyes and across his forehead and around his mouth.

"No. I can't say that I've ever been there," she acknowledged.

He looked suddenly ashamed.

The sun ducked behind a cloud outside, and the glare from the windshield of his car winked out of sight. Though he seemed harmless enough, Vickie knew the depths of cruelty that some people are capable of reaching. Her mind began flashing through possibilities of this man's secret crime. Before reaching some arbitrary verdict, however, she instead tapped the wellspring of matronly wisdom in which she'd baptized so many other lonely, wounded diners.

"I don't know what it is you've done, but I know this: guilt is a man-made ball and chain. You may want to hold on to it because it makes you feel better, like it's the punishment you deserve. But you have to let go of it."

He nodded vaguely. He was still holding the stone, rubbing a flattened portion of one side of it with his thumb. She wondered if he had eroded it for years in this manner, unconsciously thumbing it while avoiding some secret that lurked in the dark corners of his memory.

"Tell me," she said. "Tell me about this choice you've made. Maybe it's not as bad as you think."

"I don't know," he began. Instead of continuing, though, he repeated, "I don't know."

"I tell you what." She reached over and grabbed the ticket she had set in front of him. She balled it up and tossed it into the bus tub sitting on the table next to them. "Your lunch is on me today." The sun climbed out from behind the clouds and again brightened the room. "Though it may not seem like much, food is how we Southerners heal. You didn't know it, but there was salvation in that chicken sandwich."

She thought he might object to her charity, or whatever it was, but he just smiled faintly and said, "Thank you."

He turned his gaze outward once more. He still had an air of melancholy, but his expression now conveyed a sense of gratitude.

"Can I get you anything else?"

RIPPLES

He did not answer that question. When he finally did speak, the words came out thick and heavy. The story he told was indeed tragic, but by the end of it she realized that her earlier guess had been only partially right. There was more than grief in the enormous weight under which his body and soul were stooping. There was shame.

He leaned forward and laid the stone on the table with a mild clatter.

"I'm sorry, honey." She reached over and rested her hand on top of his. "I don't know what else to say after a story like that. I'm so sorry."

They sat and looked at each other in the ensuing stillness for a minute or two as the radio proffered the opening bars of the Gatlin Brothers' rendition of "It is Well." He sat back in his chair and folded his hands in his lap. His head was bowed a little, but she noticed that his back was straighter, his shoulders a little higher.

"Wait here," she said. "I've got something that may lighten that load a little more. Give me two shakes."

Before he could respond, she slipped out of the chair and carried the gray tub to the back so Gabe could finish up the lunch dishes. In the walk-in cooler, she grabbed one of the apple pies she'd baked that morning and slid it into a white box for him to take along.

Secret

When she swung back through the kitchen door, the dining room was empty. He was gone. She couldn't help but feel a little deflated that the man would leave without accepting her gift or at least saying goodbye. The clock on the wall read 3:30, which meant the dinner crew would be arriving soon. Friday afternoons always had an early crowd. She set the apple pie on the counter and went to clean up table six.

Reaching for his dessert plate and coffee mug, she was taken aback to see a one-hundred-dollar bill on the table. On top, pinning down the gracious tip, was the glassy black stone. She picked it up and realized it was much heavier than she expected. A sudden mix of sorrow and thankfulness rippled through her, and she looked out the window. The Volvo was still there. She waved at him and thrust her palm forward in a stop-sign gesture, hoping to catch him before he left so she could thank him for his generosity.

At first, Vickie could not see him through the windshield for the dazzling glare of sunlight bouncing off the glass, but it vanished again as a cloud swept in front of the sun. She waved again and started to take a step toward the door, but she stopped abruptly as she saw him staring through the window at her. If his demeanor had previously unsettled her, it now incapacitated her. He was smiling, a bewildering expression of relief and exhaustion and surrender. Watching at first with confusion, then with disbelief, then with horror, Vickie saw the man open his mouth and insert the gleaming barrel of a revolver between his teeth. She tried to scream, but the only noise she could manage to produce was a shallow, gurgling cough.

A single tear bubbled over his eyelid and slid down the side of his nose, stopping just above his lip. He heaved a shuddering breath and pulled the trigger.

For a split second, his cheeks swelled outward in a grotesque parody of a trumpet player. But the instrument at his lips was no brass horn, and he no Miles Davis.

Some part of her expected his head to explode from the violent concussion of the bullet exiting the barrel of the pistol. She thought there should be blood and brains splattered in all directions around his opened skull. Instead, there was only the brief puff of air inside his mouth and a slight upward jerk that knocked him back into an impossibly upright position with his head, still intact, leaning against the headrest for a moment. The hand with the gun dropped from sight, and a wisp of smoke trailed from his mouth. As the smoke slid upward, vanishing as it went, two thin crimson streams slid down his chin from each corner of his lips, and a

Secret

bloody cataract poured from his nose.

The scream that had lodged in her throat finally forced its way out, causing Gabe to burst through the kitchen door and into the dining room. He ran to her side and asked what was wrong. She did not answer. He tried to follow her gaze to the source of the terror that had seized her, but the sunlight had resumed its blinding reflection off the windshield and rendered the recently deceased gentleman invisible.

He slid a chair over behind her and gently guided her to sit. The cracked vinyl hissed under the weight of her body. She never took her blistered eyes from the window.

"What happened? What's wrong?"

"He's—I didn't—He—"

"He what? Who is it?"

Gabe's repeated questions produced no intelligible answers, only choked fragments and sputtered sobs. After a moment, her clenched fist opened to reveal a small black stone pressed into her palm. She turned it over in her fingers, rolling it back and forth until her thumb found an indentation on one side of it. It was almost like the groove had been made specifically for her.

Thinking it may hold some answers, Gabe reached his hand out to take the stone from her. It disappeared into her fist again, and she turned to look at him. Her usually beaming eyes were cloudy, heavy. Outside in the car, the man's body had slumped sideways against the door, free from the constraints of will and muscle that had for so long kept him upright.

    Gabe and Vickie stared at each other, one in utter bafflement, the other in wretched pain. Neither noticed that the radio had once again fallen silent.

II. Hurt

"I wish he would just *talk* to me. Not just about what to cook for dinner or to ask me if I checked the mail. All I want is to matter enough to him to have a conversation with me."

"I know how you feel. Your father would go for days without talking to me sometimes. I mean, nothing more than just, 'Where's the newspaper?' Of course, that was after—"

"Don't do that. Don't compare my marriage to yours. This is not the same thing, Mother."

"I know—"

"He's just so *stupid* sometimes. I mean, I practically have to beg him to talk to me, and when his silence sends me into a rage, he's all surprised when I lash out at him. God, I wish I could just die."

"Don't say that. You know he loves you. He just needs to learn how to show it."

"Jesus, I'm so sick of hearing that. He's not going to change. How many chances do I have to give him?"

"I'm sorry, sweetheart, I just don't know what to say."

"I've got to go. There's a call on the other line."

■ ■ ■ ■

"Hello, may I speak with Mrs. Wents?"

"Yes, this is she."

"Hi, Mrs. Wents. This is Mrs. Foster, Olivia's math teacher. How are you?"

"I'm fine. What's going on?"

"I'm sorry, I hate to make calls like this, but I need to talk to you about something. Has Olivia told you what happened at school today?"

"No, what's wrong? What's happened?"

"Well, after school, she and another student were arguing in my classroom while I was standing out in the hallway during dismissal. Maybe you know Kyle Reynolds? They've apparently been dating, or whatever they call it these days."

"Yes, I know him. What were they arguing

about?"

"I'm not sure. I usually don't get involved in things like this. You know, it just embarrasses the kids, and everything is already so awkward for them, anyway. But when I heard them arguing, I went in there to check on them, and . . ."

"And?"

"I'm sorry to have to tell you this, but she hit him."

"What do you mean? She slapped him?"

"No, ma'am. She actually punched him. In the face."

"Oh. Did she say anything?"

"She said . . . she said, 'Next time, I'll really hurt you.' I have to say, he looked pretty scared. I mean, he's bigger than she is, but the way she had him backed up against the wall and then punched him—I think it really scared him."

"Wait, what did he do?"

"He almost started crying, but when he saw me—"

"No, what did he do before she hit him? What did she mean by 'next time'?"

"Oh. I'm sorry, I didn't ask."

"Really? It seems like that's a pretty important detail. I swear, if he touched my daughter—"

"Mrs. Wents? I just wanted to let you know about what happened so you could talk to her. I

RIPPLES

know she was upset, but for her to react that way, it just worries me."

"Yeah, what worries me is that we've always tried to teach her to be strong and stand up for herself, and now she's in trouble."

"No, please don't misunderstand me. She's not in trouble. I didn't go to the principal about this because I didn't want her to be suspended or anything. He said he was okay, and she said she was sorry for hitting him. I just told them they needed to go on home. Olivia really is such a sweet girl most of the time. I've never seen her act like this before."

"I know my daughter, and I know she would never do anything to hurt someone unless there was a good reason for it."

"I'm sorry about all this, Mrs. Wents. I just wanted to let you know."

"Yeah. Thanks for the phone call, I guess."

■ ■ ■ ■

"Guess who I just off the phone with?"
"Who?"
"Mrs. Foster."
"Foster?"
"Your daughter's math teacher. Remember?"
"Oh, right. Is everything okay?"

Hurt

"Apparently, Olivia was arguing with Kyle in her room after school, and she punched him."

"Wait, what? Like in the face?"

"Yep."

"Oh, my God. Why?"

"I don't know, Mrs. Foster didn't say. She didn't even ask what was going on."

"Did Olivia say anything on the way home?"

"Not a word. She just sat there and stared out the window while Joseph talked about some movie they watched in class today, which is the second one this week, by the way. I swear, that elementary school has gone downhill ever since that idiot Cindy Rayburn took over."

"God. I wonder what made her punch him like that."

"I don't know. I'm sure he deserved it."

"Well, we should probably find out exactly what he did. Maybe it's not that bad."

"Um, your daughter just punched a boy in the face. She had to have a good reason. Mrs. Foster also told me that Olivia threatened to 'really hurt' him the next time."

"The next time what?"

"That's what I want to know. I'm going to go talk to her."

"I think we both should."

"Oh, now you suddenly want to act like you care

RIPPLES

about her, when you couldn't be bothered to take her to practice yesterday?"

"I told you I was sorry about that, but I can't skip those meetings. I have to be there every Tuesday."

"Whatever. I swear, I wish I'd married a man with a backbone. Get out of my way. I'm going to talk to my daughter."

■ ■ ■ ■

"Mom, can you *please* tell Joseph to stay out of my room. He's such a brat. I can't stand him."

"I know he's not easy to deal with, but you know how much he looks up to you."

"Whatever, I just wish he would stay out of my stuff."

"Well, that's what little brothers do. Mine were like that all the time. Anyway, that's not why I'm here. Mrs. Foster just called."

"Am I in trouble?"

"No, you're not in trouble, but she told me what happened. I need to know what's going on. What did Kyle do to you?"

"Nothing. Everything's fine."

"Wrong. Something happened that made you want to hit him. What did he do? What did you mean by 'next time'?"

Hurt

"*Nothing.*"

"You can't just sit there and not tell me. I'm your mother, and this is my job. If he hurt you in some way, you need to tell me now. Did he touch you?"

"Oh, my *God*, Mom. No."

"Are you sure? Has he tried to?"

"No, he didn't touch me. I don't want to talk about this."

"Too bad. Your teacher calls me and tells me you punched someone, and you don't want to talk about it? I need to know right now. If we need to go to that school or press charges—"

"Oh, my God. He didn't do anything. Just . . . go away!"

"Tell me right now, *what did he do?*"

"Ugh, *okay*. He didn't sit with me at lunch today."

"You better watch your tone. What happened at lunch? Why didn't he sit with you?"

"Me and Kyle always sit together, but today, he went and sat with his friend Jeremy instead."

"Did he tell you why?"

"He said they were going to talk about some stupid video game that's coming out soon. I was like, 'fine,' and he walked right over there and sat down. I can't be*lieve* he did that to me. I was *so* embarrassed."

RIPPLES

"Remember when I told you that Kyle was one of those boys who was going to treat you like crap whenever he thought something better came along? This is what I was talking about."

"He *knew* I was mad, too."

"How do you know?"

"Because I was like, *'fine,'* you know? I said it really mean to him, but he didn't even notice."

"Sweetheart, he noticed. He just didn't care. Boys are always going to do what they want, and they're going to get mad at you if you get upset about it. I'm sorry to break it to you, but every boy is like that."

"Every boy?"

"I'm afraid so."

"What about Dad?"

"Even him."

"Is that why you get so mad when he goes fishing?"

"Actually, yes. That's exactly why. He knows I don't like it, but he does it anyway. If he really loved his family, he wouldn't want to get away from us. You see what I mean?"

"Yeah. I guess that's why you hit him sometimes?"

"No, that's completely different. That's—look, I hate to tell you this, but your dad can be really selfish. I love him, but he makes me feel invisible,

Hurt

like I don't matter. So sometimes I lash out, you know? It's like he backs me into a corner and I have no choice. But you can't just punch somebody for hurting your feelings. That will get you in trouble."

"It just made me feel so stupid, and he didn't even care."

"I know. I'm sorry, sweetheart. Here, let me see your hand. Does it hurt?"

"A little."

■ ■ ■ ■

"Kyle didn't sit with her at lunch today."

"What, really? That's what this is all about?"

"That's what she told me."

"That's not exactly a capital offense. She hit him for not sitting with her at lunch?"

"He sat with his friend Jeremy instead. I can see why she was upset."

"Yeah, but is that any reason to hit him? I'm just as protective as the next dad, but I really don't think he deserved that."

"You know, you could actually take up for your daughter here. Somebody hurts her feelings, and you want to make excuses for him instead of supporting her?"

"I do support her. It's just that—"

RIPPLES

"It's just that she's a girl, which means she's irrational and stupid, right? She's just overreacting?"

"God, of course not. You know that's not what I'm saying."

"What are you saying?"

"I'm saying that . . . it's just that I don't want her using violence as a way to deal with being upset."

"You have *no* idea how hard it is to be a girl, especially at this age. The whole boy thing is bad enough, but she has to deal with the other girls on top of that. God, middle school girls are *mean*."

"Oh, I remember."

"No, you don't get it. You never had to experience it. Girls may have seemed mean to you, but they're the worst to each other. I remember Shelly Bernard being hateful to me in sixth grade because I was skinnier than her. It didn't help that she had that big nose and her face was covered in acne. Seems like her parents would have done something about that. There was a reason everyone called her Saint Bernard."

"It's a good thing they grow out of it. Imagine if adults acted that way."

"For someone as smart as you, you are so dumb. There are plenty who grow up to be just as hateful as they were in sixth grade. Remember how Susan

Hurt

supposedly 'forgot' to invite Joseph to her son's birthday party like it was some kind of accident? She's a perfect example."

"I remember. So what do we do about the situation with Kyle?"

"Well, since you didn't want to have anything to do with it, I took care of it."

"What? You told me not to go in there with you."

"Oh, so you don't have your own brain? You can't make your own choices? I guess that's my fault too, right? You can't do what you want because of your harpy wife?"

"No, that's—I thought you didn't want me in there."

"Whatever. You know, if you weren't such a coward these kids might actually respect you."

"So what did you tell her?"

"What do you think I said? I explained to her that boys are selfish jerks sometimes."

■ ■ ■ ■

"Hello, Mrs. Wents?"

"Yes, this is she."

"Hi, this is Judith Reynolds, Kyle's mom?"

"Hi, Judith. I was just about to call you."

"Yeah, I figure we need to talk about what

happened."

"Probably so. What did Kyle tell you?"

"Well, he told me that he and Olivia had a fight in Mrs. Foster's room after school and, um, Olivia punched him."

"Did he tell you why?"

"He did, and that's why I'm a little, you know, concerned. Especially considering what she said to him."

"What exactly are you concerned about? He was rude to her, and they had an argument. Honestly, I don't blame her for being upset."

"I just don't see it as that simple. It wasn't just an argument. She yelled at him for being a jerk and then punched him. And then she threatened him, said she would 'really hurt' him next time."

"I know what she said, and I know why she said it. Judith, you and I both know how men are. Kyle and Olivia may be young, but this is when they learn how they are going to be as adults. Maybe she shouldn't have hit him so hard, but don't you see she was taking up for herself? Shouldn't all girls learn to do that?"

"So hard? She shouldn't have hit him at all. Is this how you want her to act as an adult? Do you want her to think this is a healthy way to handle conflict in a relationship? You should see Kyle's face. It's not a black eye or anything, but his cheek is definitely bruised. I hope you don't think my twelve-year-old son deserves that for sitting with his friend at lunch."

"Look, Judith, I don't know what to tell you. I've already discussed this with Olivia, and I told her that this is basically what she has to look forward to when it comes to boys. It's not like I want her to go around punching everyone who makes her mad, but I have always taught her to stand up for herself. If a boy mistreats her, I don't think she should just take it."

"I'm sorry, we seem to have different definitions of 'mistreat.' Kyle didn't do anything wrong. He certainly didn't do it to be mean."

"You know, that's how women end up with men who control every aspect of their lives. It's one small compromise at a time. One false apology at a time. No one leaps into an unhappy marriage. They end up there by taking a thousand little tiny steps that don't seem to matter at the time. But one day you look around, and there you are."

"I'm sorry, are you hearing what you're saying? You basically just accused my son of being a wife beater in the making. All because of his choice of where to sit at lunch?"

"Ha, you can put words in my mouth if you want to, but I think this conversation is pretty much over. And as for our kids, I'm pretty sure they just need to stay away from each other. Good night, Judith."

"You know what, Mrs. Wents, I think that's a good idea. Good ni—"

■ ■ ■ ■

"Yeah, so that was Kyle's mom. She, of course, spent the whole time defending her poor little son. I guess he didn't feel the need to apologize for what he did. It sounded like they were just going to blame it all on Olivia."

"Honestly, I can see why she's upset. What would you say if Joseph comes home in a couple of years with a black eye? If his girlfriend hit him for hanging out with someone other than her?"

"Seriously? You are still defending *him*? You're supposed to be a *man*. How many times have I explained that you're *supposed* to take up for your family? Are you going to blame her every time some boy mistreats her? Are you going to blame her for everything?"

"No, and I know where this is headed. You need to remember something. I am not him. I'm nothing like your—"

"How did I know you were going to bring *him* up? You really know how to make a bad situation a thousand times worse, don't you? You see what you're doing, right? You're blaming this on me, on my 'daddy issues.'"

"That is not at all—"

"This is why we end up fighting. You can't wait to find something wrong with me and make me feel like garbage. It's like you're always looking for some way to tear me down a little further."

"I'm sorry, I wasn't trying to make anything worse. I certainly don't want to fight with you. Let's figure out what to do for Olivia. Maybe we should teach her some ways to handle her anger, like breathe slowly and count to ten. That may help to—"

"That is so stupid. Counting to ten doesn't work. You can't just make yourself not angry."

"That's just an example. I mean we should talk to her about being able to manage her emotions."

"Like you do? Mr. Man of Steel? Mr. Robot Man who never shows any feelings at all? Is that what you want?"

"No, I'm not a robot. I have—"

"Hey, kids! Come here a minute!"

"What are you doing?"

"I want to see what the kids think about this. About their Dear Daddy and how sensitive and emotional he is."

"No, we are not going to argue in front of—"

"Here, kids, come sit here with me. Just hop up

here on the bed. Daddy was trying to teach me something. Go ahead, Daddy."

"It's okay, you two can go back and watch TV. We're just—"

"*No.* They are going to sit right here while you explain how we should all manage our emotions."

"I'm not—"

"They're waiting."

"—going to do this in front of them."

"Why not? Why am I special? Why am I the only one who gets to see the tyrant in action? The dictator? The man who knows everything?"

"I'm not doing this."

"Oh, look, kids. Look at that. The robot doesn't have anything else to say. No words, no tears, nothing. Aww, he must be broken. He probably doesn't even love us."

"Daddy, *say* something. Please talk to us."

"It's okay, Joseph. I love you and your sister very much. Mommy and I both do. Now go back in the other room. Don't worry, everything's okay."

"Everything is *not* okay! You want to stand here and tell me that people shouldn't be angry, that they shouldn't be allowed to have their own feelings just because your heart is stone?"

"I never said—"

"You want our twelve-year-old daughter to 'manage her emotions'? So she doesn't speak her

Hurt

mind? So she doesn't stand up for herself? So she can let some jerk walk all over her and ignore her? So she'll just let him drag her across the country to some godforsaken place because his job is the most important thing in his life? I guess that makes sense. It's how you treat me, so why shouldn't she be the same way?"

"I never said that. I *never* said she shouldn't have emotions. There's nothing wrong with being angry, but there are good and bad ways to deal with it. And I don't treat you—"

"You think I'm stupid? You think I don't know what you're doing? You're not talking about her. You're talking about your evil wife! You're talking about *my* anger, right? You just don't get it, do you? Why do you think I get so angry? Huh? It's because I love you. If I didn't love you, I wouldn't get so upset when you hurt me. When you make me feel ugly and alone and insignificant!"

"You really think this is what love looks like? Kids, please go on. I promise it's okay. Mom's just upset right now, and we need to talk it out."

"Don't you *dare* talk to them like that. You always want to make me look like the bad guy, like the crazy one, but not this time. I'm not letting you do that to me anymore. They need to see the truth. They need to see the real you. They need to know how cruel you really are."

"Ha! You don't need my help. You make *yourself* look crazy. Believe me, they do see the truth. They see it every single time you get mad and start lashing out at whoever's around. You do it to me, you do it to your mom. You even do it to your own kids. Anybody but the one person who actually deserves it."

"You know what? *You're* the problem here. *You.* Everything wrong in my life is because of you."

"Wow, your dad really did a number on you. Make sure you thank him next time you speak to him. Oh, wait. How long has it been? How many years have you held this grudge? It's got to be some kind of record, even for you."

"I can't believe you—"

"Come on, kids. Let's get you guys ready for bed."

"There it is! There's the moment I've been waiting for! It's time for walking away. That's the only thing you've got, and you are *so* good at it. Go ahead, walk away from me! See where that gets you. You know what? You are *just* like my father. Those kids are going to hate you one day! You hear me? *You're going to make them hate you!*"

III. Help

[three]

"Help..." Lying face up in the grass, the gravely injured man rasped his plea through bloody, cracked lips. His ability to make any sound at all was impressive, bordering on miraculous, considering the extent of his wounds.

His potential savior—the only other person for miles around—knelt down in order to hear better. "What's that?"

"Help...me..."

For a few moments, silence hovered in the narrow space between the men's faces. They stared at each other, but neither really saw beyond his

Help

own immediate circumstance.

"Oh, I'm sorry. You didn't say 'please.'" Leaning closer, he added, *"Boy."* The *b* exploded from his lips with just enough force to produce a tiny shower of spittle, and he rose to his feet with an entirely unexpected sense of calm.

Nearby, a lone red light swept silently in unceasing circles from the dashboard of the police cruiser. James's car threw its headlights a few yards ahead into the darkness. Other than that, the roadway had no other source of illumination. There were no cars traveling back and forth, no sherbet glow of streetlights, no bright full moon in the hot summer sky. But for the whites of their eyes, both men were practically invisible. It was this cloaking blackness that precipitated the decision that would have otherwise been unthinkable.

[two]

Instead of calling for help, he paused. The planet's forward motion seemed to have reversed itself, and he felt himself lurching unsteadily from the sudden change in direction. He suddenly and simultaneously felt the exhilaration of considering his options and the onerous responsibility of weighing the consequences.

RIPPLES

Everything he knew, everything he felt, everything he wanted was backward. His hand was curled around the radio handset. A man, a human being not so different from himself, lay gasping for air, pleading for help, praying for relief only a few feet away. And yet, he felt no pity or compassion. He found no sympathy for the sufferer. Instead, he discovered hatred. From boyhood, he had been taught to camouflage his hate behind polite silence and ironed smiles. He had learned the skill so well that he often forgot the hate was there. Now, however, it simmered in his bowels, then it rose boiling into his chest until it climbed white-hot into his eyes.

Another pair of headlights crested the hill and descended toward the roadside carnage. The oncoming car veered into the left lane out of deference for the radiating police light, slowing only slightly as it passed. It drove on into oblivion, and the two men were left alone again under the dire weight of an increasingly urgent choice.

The man on the ground behind him moaned. He listened to the pitiful sounds wafting through the night air, barely audible above the grinding cicadas. With his thumb on the button and hate in his throat, he stood motionless while the world careened around him.

A sudden, sharp voice burst through the radio's

Help

speaker and startled him. He dropped the handset and jumped backward. The dispatcher scratched out a series of barely intelligible words, answered immediately by an equally incoherent patrolman. The radio fell silent once more, but he retreated another step, then another.

Behind him, he heard a cough.

"H e l p . . ."

[one]

Texas State Trooper Richard T. Johnson grinned. He leaned one hand on the roof of the car so he could look down on the young motorist he'd pulled over.

From the driver's seat, James looked up at the officer leaning on his car, carefully keeping his hands in plain sight on the steering wheel. In the light of the setting sun, James could see the little brown flecks of tobacco wedged between his yellow teeth and a thin film of saliva pooling above his bottom lip.

"You know why I stopped you?" the trooper twanged.

"No, sir," James answered.

Trooper Johnson turned his head to the left, toward the front of the car, and spat loudly. Without even looking, James knew that the

RIPPLES

diarrhea-colored stream was now running down his front fender.

"C'mon now, you must've known you was doin' at least semty mile-a-hour through this here fit-ty-five mile-a-hour zone. That's a mighty big hurry for a quiet Mundy evenin' like this." He ejected another mouthful of tobacco juice to indicate that his drawled accusation was finished.

"No, sir. I had no idea I was going so fast. See, I didn't even know this old hunk could even get up to that speed." He tried to cough up a sheepish, self-conscious chuckle.

Trooper Johnson bent his tall, wiry body at the waist and rested his crossed arms in the open window. The sleeves of his uniform hitched up slightly as he did so, and James could see the gleam of pale white skin above the tan line on his left arm. Johnson's enormous mouth had flattened into a tight, humorless horizontal line, all but invisible below his mustache.

"Don't you go tellin' stories now. I *know* you know how fast you was goin' cause I seen you hit the brakes when you saw me settin' there. Ain't that right?"

James recognized the dangerous tenor of the conversation and tried to keep his balance. "Yes, sir, I did hit my brakes, but—"

"But?" The patrolman sneered. "But what? You

Help

hit the brakes cause you was speedin' like a wetback through the Rio Grandy."

"Sir, I hit my brakes cause I was coming down the hill, then I saw you and—"

"Attaboy! Now we're tellin' the truth." His grin had returned.

James knew that he had no choice. He was fully aware his '66 Plymouth could never safely reach seventy miles per hour, but he was entirely at the mercy of Trooper Johnson. He would simply have to admit his guilt and accept the ticket.

"I'm real sorry, officer. I shouldn'ta been speedin'." He had to be careful not to sound *too* apologetic, lest the esteemed law enforcement representative leaning on his car think he was being less than genuine. He knew how to walk the tightrope of contrition before white authority, but even the most skillful show of remorse could tip too far one way or the other.

"Well, ain't that sumpn. You 'real sorry' for breakin' the law here on my highway, huh? I reckon that's good enough for me. I 'spect you learned a real valliable lesson this evenin'. Ain't no need for a ticket cause you won't be drivin' like a maniac no more, 'zat about right?"

Trooper Johnson seemed to believe he was clever, as if he could trick James into thinking he was going to drive away with just a warning.

RIPPLES

"Nossir, I ain't tryin' to get away from a ticket. I know I done wrong and I gotta pay for it."

In the back of his mind, James knew that his father would be disgusted by the subtle shift in his language. However, he also knew that any semblance of eloquence was actually a liability in a situation such as this.

"Oh?" he snarled. "Now you gonna sit there and tell me how to do my job?"

"Nossir, I—"

"Look here, I don't need nobody, certainly nobody like *you*, to tell me what I need to do."

"Sir—"

"You interrup' me one more time," Trooper Johnson warned, "I'm gonna have to ask you to step outside the car."

James knew precisely what that would entail, but it was only by a heroic effort of silence that he avoided escalating the ridiculous tension any further.

Johnson smirked. "Now, I guess I can continue. If you wanna ticket so bad, I s'pose I could oblige you. There's just one little problem: you didn't say 'please.'" He leaned a little closer and added with unmistakable venom, "*Boy.*"

James didn't even wince. He'd been called "boy" nearly every day of his life. Though he hated the term with every cell in his black body, he knew

Help

well enough not to give any sign that he even noticed. Right now, the knuckle-dragging cop was scrutinizing his face for any glimpse of offense or objection, for any reason to pull James out of the car. He appeared to be practically lusting for the chance to teach this young buck about respect for the law.

For the moment, however, James held his ground. He knew he had to work up the awful courage to betray everything he believed and everything he felt by apologizing to Trooper Johnson and asking him to write a ticket. The absurdity of this game weighed heavily on James, who had begun more and more to feel like Sisyphus, forever pushing his blackness uphill only to have it roll back down just before reaching the top.

"Sir, I'm very sorry—"

But James was never able to finish his loathsome sentence, for Trooper Johnson was no longer standing at his window. In the time it had taken for James to swallow his pride and begin his apology, a car had come over the hill behind them and coasted downward without any sign of perceiving the traffic stop in progress. By the time Trooper Johnson noticed the oncoming threat, it was too late. He jumped backward just as the bumper found his left leg below his knee, and his body slammed against the hood with a sickening chorus of snaps and cracks and rolled up the windshield. For a few seconds, he was airborne, sailing half-conscious through the night air until he landed on the scrubby shoulder of the highway.

From James's perspective, there was no slow motion or sensory delay. One moment, Trooper Johnson stood beside James's car, and the next moment, his body lay some fifteen feet away, just beyond the reach of the headlights. A few yards farther down the road, the assaulting vehicle had come grinding to a halt. It was canted slightly toward the road. The door opened, and the driver stumbled out. The shape staggered forward a few steps, walking as if the ground were pitching about like a boat in rough surf. James could just make out the woman's body, but her face was still shrouded by the night. A second figure, also a woman but younger than the first, emerged from the passenger side. She ran and grabbed the frozen driver's arm and began pulling her back toward the car.

"Mother, let's go! Come on!"

For a brief second, James could see the terrified face of the older woman as she took a step toward Trooper Johnson's motionless body and into the beam of his headlights. The sound of her daughter's voice and the tugging on her arm

Help

seemed to penetrate through the drunken fog. She turned and lurched back to the car sitting askew on the side of the road. And as quickly as it had appeared, it was gone.

A minute or so passed while James struggled to process the sudden change in circumstance. The man he had so loathed and feared only moments before was now incapacitated, possibly even dead—cut down by a careless, inebriated woman.

He finally climbed out of his car and walked toward the immobile Trooper Johnson. James initially believed him to be dead, for there was no sign of any movement or any sound. As he approached, however, he was able to discern the shallow rise and fall of the officer's damaged rib cage with each ragged breath. James turned and ran to the police cruiser. He reached through the open window and pulled the radio handset from its cradle.

[four]

The taillights of a 1966 Plymouth Valiant briefly bathed half of Trooper Richard T. Johnson's sallow face in a rosy glow, then faded away as the car accelerated onto the highway, leaving in its wake a cloud of dust and consequences. The stars continued their silent vigil above as the red light in

RIPPLES

the patrol car spun on and on in tireless, indifferent circles.

IV. Ripples

My father always blamed Lucy, my older sister. Dad had instructed her to watch over me and my twin brother, but we were notoriously difficult to supervise. She always resented being stuck with us. I can't say I blame her. Grant and I made it our mission to sneak away from her at every opportunity. Still, it really wasn't her fault, what happened to Grant. It was mine. I've just never had the courage to tell anyone the truth.

Every year when we were kids, Dad took the three of us camping. We'd spend a week during the summer in the Ozarks, set up right next to the river—fishing, canoeing, exploring. For me and

RIPPLES

Grant, it was heaven. Lucy, well, she hated it. Hated every minute of it.

The last year we went, when Grant and I were ten, I snuck away early one morning to do some solo exploring. I found this pond almost a mile away from our camp that was nearly invisible through the thick growth around it. It was kind of a teardrop shape with a large granite outcropping that jutted out just over the surface of the water above the tapered end. I grabbed a handful of pebbles and climbed up onto the enormous stone. I tried to skip them but failed miserably. After that, I settled for trying to find the deepest spot by tossing one at a time and listening to each *ploop*.

Later that day, I brought Grant back to see my discovery. We sat on the edge of that huge stone and watched the fish dart back and forth for a long time. Water striders skimmed along the surface and dragged tiny trails of wake behind them. Dragonflies zipped around and lit on the ends of tall weeds that grew thick along the waterline. It was really beautiful.

As I collected more rocks, Grant insisted on inspecting each one. He had recently taken an interest in geology, largely because he had discovered our father's old rock tumbler in the garage. When he decided that I had found nothing of interest, he gave them back and struck out to

Ripples

look for more valuable minerals.

I resumed lobbing one rock after another and watching the concentric circles chase each other. It eventually dawned on me what I found so beguiling about something so mundane. No matter where the rock landed, as long as it was thrown hard enough, the perfectly circular ripples always managed to reach every inch of the water's irregular edge. If I wanted to disturb a butterfly perched on one bank, I could hit the water on the opposite side and watch the waves send it flying away. If I wanted to produce chaos across the entire surface, I could toss a handful of stones in the middle. If I wanted the entire ecosystem to reach equilibrium, I could simply sit still and wait.

Grant came back empty-handed, and I had run out of ammunition. We poked around the edge looking for whatever wildlife we could find until we surprised a water snake curled up on a fallen log. Its gray body slid into the pond and disappeared from sight in one quick motion, which sent us scurrying back to the campsite. We both pretended we weren't scared, but neither of us was very convincing to the other.

For the next couple of days, any spare moment we could steal was spent navigating back to the pond and wandering along the bank looking for any sort of artifact that would excite the imagination of a couple of ten-year-old boys. We figured there had to be any number of arrowheads or musket balls or Civil War bayonets just under the surface of the weeds and the mud. What we found were a few discarded Coke bottles and beer cans and a lot of disappointment. It was along the trail we had been slowly taming that Grant made a truly remarkable discovery. We didn't know it at the time, but it would eventually change everything.

On the third or fourth day, he stopped suddenly and squatted down by the edge of the path en route to the pond. He held up a jagged piece of what seemed to be charcoal, only it was hard and glossy. It was like nothing else we had seen on any previous expedition. He declared that it was obsidian and insisted that it was extremely rare in that particular area. Indeed, when we returned to the campsite and showed our father, he was stunned and impressed. When we told him where we found it, however, I accidentally let slip the secret of the hidden pond. His eyes flashed with what I thought must be anger at first, but his terse response belied fear.

"Don't go there again. It's too dangerous."

That was all he said. Using our collective imagination, we conjured up a dozen various possibilities for the mortal threats he could have had in mind. Mass murderers, rabid bears, everything but the obvious one.

The next time we were able to sneak away, we went straight for the forbidden pond. It was familiar territory, but now it held an all-new thrill for us. Grant and I approached with all the stealth we could, watching with vigilant eyes for any sign of dangerous creatures or psychotic kidnappers. Like our earlier attempts to find historically significant treasures, the careful search proved to be a failure. After exhausting all possibilities for adventure, I lay on my back on the warm granite and watched the clouds sweep over the clearing.

Grant opted to climb a pine tree that leaned precariously outward over the water. He shimmied up the trunk with surprising ease until he reached a limb that he could pull himself over and sit on. I yelled for him to be careful, but this only prompted him to slide farther out. I can still see the foolish grin on his face. I repeated my warning, trying very hard to sound as casual as possible to prevent him from taking any further unnecessary risk.

Nevertheless, he inched his way a little closer to the edge until the sagging branch cracked. It didn't break right away, but his devilish grin vanished. For the first time ever, I saw terror in my brother's face. He sat really still for a moment, then began to scoot back toward the trunk of the tree.

The next crack was followed by a sudden downward motion as the branch began to give way. Grant fell backward but somehow managed to hold on with one hand as the backs of his knees instinctively curled around the branch as well. He struggled to right himself. The thick clump of green needles on the end of the limb slapped down onto the water, and I thought he would be next. Instead, the supple pine split only halfway through, causing Grant and the bough to swing toward the trunk just close enough for him to land safely, albeit awkwardly, on solid ground.

I realized then that I had not moved since before the whole ordeal began. Though he had only faced a drop of about five or six feet into water that he could probably stand up in, I had been utterly paralyzed by fear. Had he been in any real danger, I suppose I would have watched him die before my eyes in a state of immobile panic. This realization sprouted a kind of shame that I could never quite uproot. It grew and bore its rotten fruit over and over again throughout the remainder of my childhood and burrowed deep into my adult psyche. Though it lay dormant for months or even years at a time, it would occasionally shoot up into full maturity in a matter of seconds, usually at the worst possible moments.

Ripples

After lying on the ground a few seconds, Grant breathed a few relieved sighs and began giggling uncontrollably. I watched him stand and brush off the dirt and pine needles clinging to his jeans. My first impulse was to scream at him, but what came out was laughter. Somehow our twin brains had reconvened, and we roared in unison. We stopped only when we heard our father's acrid voice behind us.

"Get your butts back to your tent," he said. "*Now*."

He and Lucy had followed our path after realizing we'd disappeared again, and whatever anger had seeded his earlier warning was now in full bloom. Grant dropped his chin to his chest and marched forward in resolved silence, preparing for what he assumed was going to be certain death. I followed him with my eyes glued to his heels. No one spoke the entire way back to the campsite, but Lucy's smug grin practically echoed around us. That night, rather than wearing us out with a switch, our dad struck us with a blow far more painful than any we could have imagined.

"Go and pack up everything except what you're wearing. We're leaving in the morning. You two cannot be trusted."

I remember our mouths hanging open, no protest, no pleas for mercy or understanding. We burned with indignation and childlike fury, not realizing that those feelings were just easier substitutes for remorse. Later, while we sat sulking in our tent and stoking the embers in our hearts, I thought briefly of plotting some elaborate and humble apology. After all, if our father could see that we were indeed very sorry for what we had done and that we could really be trusted, he might retract his terrible sentence. However, Grant's quiet sniffling rekindled my anger, and I discarded the idea.

The following morning, while Dad was getting everything packed up, he asked Lucy to keep an eye on us so he could get all of our supplies into the station wagon without interruption. She rolled her eyes and mumbled some sort of agreement. Under ordinary circumstances, we would've immediately schemed an escape, but we simply sat by the edge of the river and picked at the moss growing nearby.

Grant's voice finally broke the silence.

He told me, "This is all your fault."

I said, "What?"

I guess my confusion upset him further. He snapped, "You heard me. This is your fault."

"What's my fault?" I asked.

He glared with his steely eyes and said, "Everything, stupid. We're leaving and probably never coming back because of *you*. You and that stupid pond."

I responded with, "Who's stupid? You went with me. I didn't make you go."

This didn't make any difference. He maintained my guilt: "Yeah, but you found it. If you hadn't gone there in the first place, we never would have gotten in trouble." He folded his arms across his chest, and his eyes smoldered with genuine resentment. I'll never forget that hateful glare. Everything about his posture, facial expression, and tone of voice exuded a confidence that could only exist behind bulletproof logic. My culpability was a rational and moral certainty from which I could never recover.

Still, I tried one last time. "We didn't get in trouble because I found it. We got in trouble because we went back after Dad said not to. This isn't *my* fault."

"I hate you and I wish you were dead," he declared, and with that, he sealed himself up in his stubbornness and ignored all my attempts to defend myself. He pulled the hunk of obsidian from his pocket, pretending to inspect it as a signal that he was done listening to me. Where I had initially felt sadness that my twin brother had basically renounced me, I now felt rage. It was an entirely new sensation for me, a blissful pain that burned in my chest and behind my eyes. In place of my usually gentle nature, I found a desire to hurt Grant the way he hurt me. No, worse. I wanted to destroy some part of him that he couldn't get back. I was bigger and stronger, but a physical beating was too temporary.

Without a word, I stood up and loomed over him like I was about to pummel him. His shoulders slumped a little, almost imperceptibly, but not quite. He feigned disinterest and kept turning that black lump over and over in front of his face. When I reached out to snatch it, he flinched, trying to avoid a blow that was never coming. Before he even knew I had his precious rock, I was already plunging into the opening in the trees that led to the pond. In my haste, I failed to notice that Lucy had entered her tent to change clothes, and Dad's head was buried in the back of the station wagon. Neither of them saw me or Grant leave the safety of the riverbank.

I ran through the woods with ease, twisting and turning without even having to think about where I was going. My head-start and slightly longer legs meant that by the time my brother caught up to me, I was standing on the granite dais with my most sadistic smile. He was about to demand that I return the rock to him, but he fell silent when he saw the rippling movement of the water behind me. Tears pooled in his eyes. There was no anger

Ripples

at all, just grief, like his best friend in the world had died. I had expected to feel something in that moment, some kind of resolution to the hatefulness that had compelled my cruelty. I wanted to feel victorious, but the look of agony on his face turned all my rage into regret. The awful irony was that I had succeeded beyond my expectation.

I remember saying to him, "Hey, I'm sorry. Look, I didn't—"

But I never finished that sentence. Even to this day, I have never spoken the last few words. It was too late. Grant had bolted up the inclined stone past me and jumped blindly into the murky water. His aim was true; he landed squarely in the spot where I had broken the stillness of the pond only moments before. I shouted for him, but I choked on his name and did nothing but watch the enormous rings of water pulsing from the center of his dive. I watched as the surface of that pond slowly returned to its flat, calm state. It was like I had become part of the granite fixture under my feet. I stood with my eyes fixed on the glassy water, waiting for Grant to surface. Waiting for my brother to be okay.

I still don't know how long it took for Dad and Lucy to arrive in the clearing, how long I had stood there, looking stupidly at the water. Their initial questions had no effect on me at all.

RIPPLES

Where is Grant?
Did he go in the water?
Where is he?

What finally broke the spell was watching my father's body hit the water, which sent the reflection of the sky and trees into a wobbling frenzy. He disappeared into the darkness and resurfaced every so often. Again and again he dove, rising for air then back down again.

I finally heard Lucy's panicked voice: *David, what happened?*

I could only answer in clips and fragments. *I don't know—he didn't say anything—I didn't hear the splash—I looked for him, but—I don't know.*

I'd like to think that the lies were unconscious, that I didn't really know what I was saying. But I knew.

When my father pulled Grant's body from the water, his right arm was covered up to the elbow with slick black mud. Later, he said the arm was wedged underneath a fallen tree trunk six feet below the surface, like he was digging around underneath it and had gotten stuck. No one had any explanation for it, no way to guess what he could have been searching for.

I never told them what I did. I never told them what he said to me or that I pretended to throw his rock in the water. I never told them that it was in my pocket the whole time. I never told them anything. I couldn't. At first, it was panic. I lied because I didn't know what would happen to me. Over time, the lie turned to stone. It became the truth to everyone else, and I couldn't undo it. If I ever told them the truth, it would be like digging up his body and killing him again in front of them. If I ever told the truth, I would have to admit that I murdered him, and that I did it for spite.

But I did. I murdered Grant. In a stupid, blind fit of childish rage, I threw him into six feet of cold, muddy water and drowned him. It took a long time for me to understand that I hadn't just killed my brother. I had thrown a grenade right in the middle of my family, and every one of us took some shrapnel. We were all still alive, but none of us really survived. We all stopped going to church. Sundays just didn't feel holy anymore. I wrapped myself in secrecy and denial. Dad threw himself into his work. Mom grieved herself into an alcoholic haze. Lucy lost herself in a string of boyfriends.

Lucy. Like I said, my father blamed her. He tolerated her presence, but I don't remember ever seeing him speak to her again. He piled his guilt on top of her own and suffocated her. When she finally left for college, she disappeared into the world and never returned. Every now and then, I would see a

RIPPLES

letter from her in Mom's desk drawer. I never read them.

I've never told anyone this story, not even my wife. I probably should have, but it's too late for that. Sometimes I think a secret is like a rotten tooth. You can hide it for a while, maybe for a long time, but it'll eventually begin to poison you from the inside. It's like the truth wants to get out, and if it doesn't, it will kill you. Maybe that's why I'm telling you all this, I don't know. It's like I've carried this thing around for so long that I didn't know how to let go of it. But I have to. I can't hold on to it anymore. After all these years, I guess I just needed to tell the truth to someone—to anyone—so I can finally put it down.

V. Ants

Jordan sat on the driveway watching his daughter ride her bike up and down the asphalt in the streaky summer twilight. The training wheels rattled and squeaked as she pedaled with all the might her tawny legs could muster. She scratched to a stop in front of Jordan, and he smiled at her.

"You're doing great. It's almost time to lose those training wheels."

She grinned and climbed down from the bike. The little girl with dusty blonde curls plopped in her father's lap, wiping the trace of sweat from her forehead on his sleeve. He pointed to an ant crawling by his leg.

RIPPLES

"Look. See that ant? There's a smaller ant clamped onto his leg, and they've been fighting for the last few minutes. The big one can't seem to shake the little one."

"His name is Big Ant," she said, pointing her finger. "That one's name is Little Ant."

The childlike simplicity made Jordan smile. He had always known he would enjoy being a father, but he had no way of knowing how much it was possible to love another person.

"Daddy, why are they fighting?"

"I don't know. What do you think ants fight about?" As a man of science, he had the habit of turning questions back on his daughter.

"Maybe they can't share their toys."

Jordan laughed. "Maybe. Sounds familiar, huh?" He gave her a playful poke in the ribs, which elicited a giggle. It was probably the purest sound he knew.

"Or maybe they hate each other," she offered. "Like you and Mommy." Her words, though spoken in the matter-of-fact tone so natural to children, scalded him.

"Mommy and I don't hate each other, sweetie. We get mad sometimes, sort of like you get mad at your brother, but that's not for you to worry about. All grown-ups do it. The important thing is we both love you so much."

Ants

Together, Jordan and his little girl watched the ants grapple for several more minutes. There was much fury but no progress in any direction. Big Ant stumbled blindly around in circles, pausing occasionally to try and dislodge Little Ant's jaws from his leg. For a minute or so, they stopped completely, but then their combat resumed with increased fervor. Jordan studied their movements carefully. He, too, wondered why they fought, and he couldn't help but note the futility of their struggle. There was no way for either of them to win; they were bound to their quarrel—and bound to each other by it. He looked up just in time to see a shadow disappear behind the curtains. It was almost time for the kids to take baths. He kissed the girl on her head, but she was so rapt by the battle raging around her toes that she took no notice.

"Daddy, do we look like ants to God?"

This question startled Jordan. "Maybe," he said, obviously unsure of how to answer such a query. Many of his family members talked about God regularly, and they took the kids to church on special occasions. She had learned about God and Jesus in a very distant manner, but this was the first time she had acknowledged any recognition of a deity without any ceremonial attachments. He was amazed by the depth of the question, amazed

RIPPLES

that a five-year-old was trying to understand the nature of God's perspective relative to people.

Jordan looked back down at the ants. Maybe if there were a God, this is how He would see us. We would probably appear as mindless insects, fighting each other for no conceivable purpose. Creatures who move without meaning, build without growing, live without seeing. But Big Ant soldiered on, unaware of his omniscient observer. He had a reason, temporary as it was, to free himself from the jaws of Little Ant. His life depended entirely on escaping, and after that, there was still only the goal of survival. Jordan could certainly sympathize. He wrapped his arms around the tiny human snuggled in his lap. She smelled delicately of sweat.

As if cued by an unseen director, she jumped up and climbed back onto her bike, the pendulum of her attention span swinging back toward the need for motion. Jordan picked up a twig and carefully pinned down Little Ant by his fat, bulbous rear end. He thought of God's enormous cosmic hand arbitrating in the affairs of men; was there any justice in divine intervention? If God really created the universe and its inhabitants, then the laws of nature inevitably enforced His will and left men without any chance of true freedom. They could live and work and love, totally unconscious of the fated paths indelibly laid before them. And in the end, all could be swept away at random by a single act of some distant being.

Little Ant squirmed under the pressure, but his jaws remained clenched. Big Ant, unsure of the implications of this new development, fought even more ferociously. His efforts succeeded in wrenching Little Ant's body apart, the head and thorax torn away from the abdomen, which now lay inert under the stick in Jordan's hand. Still, Little Ant's mouth clutched his opponent's leg, unyielding.

Jordan looked up into the summer Tuesday twilight and watched the fireflies flashbulb their love songs along the edge of the trees. He was suddenly grateful for the empty expanse of space beyond the smeared reds and oranges of the atmosphere. No invisible judge watched him, no hand ready to pin him down. If Jordan could not rescue one stupid ant from the jaws of another, how could any God possibly work in the lives of so many stupid human beings? Maybe that was the wrong question. How could God even know what needed to be done? Maybe Jordan had chosen the wrong side; Little Ant very well could have been the victim of some tragic mistreatment and was fighting for a just cause. Maybe—

A tearful shriek whipped Jordan's head around.

RIPPLES

Bicycle and rider had overturned, the training wheel bent at the axle, still spinning.

He jumped to his feet and scooped up his daughter and reassured her.

"It's okay, sweetie. I've got you."

A thin trail of blood seeping from her skinned elbow trickled down onto Jordan's forearm as he carried her toward the house to clean the wound. She buried her face into her father's warm shirt to dry her tears. In the fading dusk, Big Ant stumbled around, still unable to free his defunct leg from the dying clutches of his adversary.

VI. Gone

Amid the shards of glass strewn around like flat, translucent teeth, Marcie lay motionless on the blacktop of I-5, a few miles north of Seattle. With her cheek pressed against the cold asphalt, she fixed her eyes on a triangular piece of the exploded windshield a few inches away. It was sort of Kentucky-shaped, but that might just be a bit of grade school geography curriculum infiltrating her consciousness to distract her from the present chaos. No, it definitely bore the shape of Kentucky: roughly triangular with a bulge in one side and a flat margin opposite. The man on the radio had said only a few moments before that the current temperature was fifty-four degrees, but it would

RIPPLES

drop within a few hours as the rain blew in. She managed to swallow a little, her eyes still affixed to that irregular shard. She did not yet register the absence of her left leg just above the knee.

For the moment, she was spared the agony of severed nerves and rent tissue, and though she lay blissfully unaware, the blood poured in dark, steady rivulets from the ragged stump. Nearby, the rear wheels of her inverted car finally exhausted their inertia and stopped spinning. One headlight was torn from its housing, but the other still cast its perfectly aligned beam. It did little more in the gray dusk than illuminate the particles of dust that were beginning to settle in the aftermath of the accident.

I need to call the bakery again and verify the order for tomorrow, Marcie thought.

The sounds around her began to force their way into her consciousness, but not all at once. First, a steady roar from the traffic on the overpass nearby. Then a voice—no, two voices—very close. Sirens, distant but rising in pitch, two or three in frustrating disharmony. A steady drumbeat in her chest.

I hope those books arrived. They should have been here Tuesday. They're already two days late.

Footsteps crunching, hard soles on glass and gravel. A mosquito whining right past her ear, or maybe a motorcycle flying down the on-ramp. Her own breathing.

I wonder how he's doing, she thought. *Is he happy?*

That particular question arose periodically, peeking timidly out from behind all the concrete barriers she had erected around the memory of her husband's departure. It remained unexplored and unanswered, always shoved back into captivity by the more prudent custodians of her mind.

Rubber-gloved hands grabbed her and rolled her over, ripping her clothing and exploring her injuries as red and blue lights splintered the air around her. There were voices, too, but they came and went as if synchronized with the dancing lights.

Is he still in town? Did he take another . . .

The words slipped away into some kind of neuronal void, a mental abyss formed by the steady loss of oxygen to her brain. Then there was blackness. But Marcie was still quite conscious, aware of the dark veil over her eyes, still feeling the hands on her body, the straps pulled across her thighs and chest, the bounce of the gurney rolling into the ambulance.

Over the years, she had become accustomed to the emptiness of the house, the silence that collected like dust in the corners, long before he actually left. It wasn't his absence that grieved her—*how can you feel something that isn't there?*—it was the unanswered questions he left behind. Somewhere in the darkness above her, voices spoke in clipped codes and abbreviations over the accompaniment of a siren. Her name floated across the haze.

Marcie Anderson.

I guess I should change it back to my maiden name.

She had been half of Captain and Mrs. Anderson for as long as she could remember, and the fragmentary remains of her former self played just beyond her memory's reach.

When she arrived home every evening, she hung her keys on the hook by the door. There were two hooks, actually, mounted under a giant whimsical *A* carved out of wood that her brother had given them as a wedding present. It was not necessarily stylish or even well crafted, but she had loved it. Now, as her key ring dangled there, it was conspicuously alone. His hook remained empty all the time, a frequent reminder of the man she had amputated from her life.

Maybe I could have done more.

Her body, still strapped to the gurney, lurched to the left as the ambulance made a hard turn. An EMT cursed the sudden loss of balance.

Gone

Or maybe he could have been honest.

She should probably get rid of the his/hers key hooks, but something about it just wouldn't let her.

A decade of memories, homogenized by repetition and routine, swam across the edge of her vision. Ten years, four homes, a handful of Air Force bases. The bases were all exactly the same, but each house were special. The stone fireplace in the Tacoma house, the brittle lawn of the Wichita Falls house, original hardwood floors in Boston, a clawfoot tub in Belleville.

I would kill to take one more bath in that tub.

Moving vans and the decayed smell of cardboard boxes. Tearful farewell hugs and awkward introductory handshakes.

He transferred at every opportunity. Other officers found ways to stay in one place for five or six years at a time, but not Captain Anderson. Every two years, they moved on to a new town, a new base, the same pattern. They were always moving and never going anywhere, like he was running from something, or perhaps looking for something.

The ambulance braked, probably approaching an intersection. It didn't stop, just slowed enough to give Marcie the impression that gravity had been turned on its side and she was now falling horizontally.

RIPPLES

We were a handsome couple.

They were indeed, especially draped in the formality of black-tie events. He in dress blues with iceberg eyes, she in a black evening gown with swept-up chestnut curls. Dinings-in were her favorite because she got to see him laugh.

Did he laugh at the wedding?

It wasn't infidelity. At every new post, gossipy base-wives regaled her with stories about cheating husbands and the relentless forgiveness cycle, but Marcie never once doubted her husband's faithfulness.

I never was a jealous woman, she thought. *Should I have been?*

He had always carried something with him, a considerable pressure that left him exhausted and joyless. Though they were thousands of miles apart, every house felt haunted by the same presence, a plaintive cry that was palpable but never quite audible.

What was it? Why couldn't he ever tell me?

The voices above her now chirped and squawked like a tree full of birds terrorized by some unseen predator. They had increased in intensity, and Marcie smiled (or thought she smiled) at their ridiculous tone. All that fuss about nothing.

Most of his time was spent at work. Whatever

Gone

job he actually did was classified, so they never talked about it when he came home.

What did we talk about? The weather?

They talked about many things. In the rare moments they had together, they discussed politics, movies, restaurants. He always spoke to her in calm, quiet measures. A soft, deep voice that embraced her. But then he was gone, even on weekends. Maybe playing golf or hunting or camping—she had never really been sure. Not that she minded. She rather enjoyed the freedom to move about from room to room in her own house, opening whatever doors she pleased and turning lights on and off. She would sit and read for hours while he was away.

I'm not sure he even owned a book. Could that be right?

Most nights she curled up on the loveseat with the echoing silence around her like a shawl, with the pages full of words, the words full of breath.

The ambulance screeched a little as it stopped in front of the ER. The birds and their voices overhead were suddenly farther away.

Finally, I can get some rest.

Then she and the gurney were spat out onto the sidewalk, where they were greeted by a different species of sounds.

Maybe not.

RIPPLES

By all accounts, Captain Anderson was a kind man, very thoughtful and mannerly. Polite almost to a fault, which she had pointed out a couple of times. Of course, it didn't bother him, and that was kind of the problem. They never argued, he never shouted, she never nagged. Not that she wanted to fight with him, but his infinitely even-keeled manner disquieted her. It was like he was missing something, some part of him that would engage if he could just upset the balance a little bit.

He buried himself under that uniform. The military gave him the perfect place to hide.

When she filed the papers, he had signed them without blinking. There was plenty of money to share. No debts, no children. Neither of them shed a tear. And with that, he was gone. The bonds of matrimony severed by ink and paper, a clean, surgical operation. It was more like losing a comfortable pair of jeans than losing a husband.

Is he happy now?

He had hugged her goodbye after packing up his few belongings and loading the car. Strange how she could still feel his tight chest pressing gently against her ear, stranger still that she barely felt it at the time. She wanted to know what was in there, wanted to locate the tumor that had wrapped its tendrils around his heart and squeezed it flat.

Gone

The gurney rumbled and jostled down a hallway, then another, and another. The birds were gone, replaced evidently by a tribe of pagans who muttered and chanted around her in low tones. Marcie suddenly realized that the emergency contact information on her chart was probably still his. Would they call him?

Would he come? Would he—

The question was cut short by a scorching pain in her left leg, right about where the knee should have been. There were other injuries—contusions, lacerations, fractures—but their alarms were silenced by the screams of her disembodied limb. The agony washed over her and dissolved all the light and sound around her until the cool darkness carried her away.

VII. Shells

As the breakers hissed around his ankles, the old man shuffled along the sand. Every few steps, he stopped and leaned over to look at a shell. Most of them were cracked and splintered, on their way to being ground up into the same particles that covered all the beaches along the southeastern coast. He'd examine each one for a moment, then sometimes flip it over with his walking stick for a better look. The stick, a piece of driftwood nearly as tall as he was, about five feet in length and over an inch thick, had all but become an extension of himself. He had etched his name in block letters near the top: LOYD. Its bark had been long discarded, and it had been smoothed and polished by years of exposure to sand and salt.

Shells

His skin, however, was anything but smooth. Like most other beach-dwellers of his age, he was covered in deep, brown wrinkles.

After his wife passed, he had traded her companionship for that of the much brighter, less forgiving South Carolina sun. They had talked often of retiring to the low country, of spending their last years together among the salt marshes and sea islands, but her body had succumbed early to decades of grief and gin. In a way, she was lucky to have buried only one of their children, he thought. The fat and muscle of his youth seemed to have given way to wires and sinews that now barely propped him up. It was almost as if he'd been preserved by desiccation, worn down to a taxidermied skeletal frame. An expression of vague but persistent disapproval began in a furrow between his eyes and descended in sharp lines to the creases around his mouth.

His walks were as regular as the tides. In fact, he followed the charts with as much precision as his body and the weather would allow. One hour after high tide, twice a day, he would take his stick and cross the boardwalk spanning the dunes behind his home. At the bottom of the stairs that led down to the beach, he would turn right and begin his hunt. As the tide retreated, it left behind thousands of specimens for him to evaluate.

RIPPLES

The old man knew the ocean's vocabulary well. He recognized the scallops and cockles and whelks by name and by sight. The clams alone required their own lexicon: quahog, razor, Venus, coquina. An ever-present layer of periwinkles crackled under his sandals while he made his one-mile trek toward the mouth of the inlet.

Inevitably, his solitary walk was punctuated by the squeals of children and the admonishing shouts of their parents. As peaceful as it was, this stretch of beach was also a treasured destination for tourists. Even in the colder months, the old man would still have to dodge a family or two to make his daily journeys. In the summer, his beach was invaded by vacationing hordes who plundered the shoreline, taking whatever living or dead specimens they wanted. He would watch as toddlers and teens ran amok, poking at horseshoe crabs and taunting sea gulls. Lobster-red dads cast their lines into the surf to catch sharks or hunted in the tidal pools for blue crabs. Moms in their modest, skirted one-pieces strolled with buckets, bags, and nets, collecting all the shells they could find. It didn't matter how many they had; there was always another and another and another.

And so he plodded on, day after day, searching for the shells that were still intact. He found them beautiful, and he was captivated by the balance

Shells

between delicacy and resiliency. Most were thin and brittle, cracking under the slightest pressure, yet so many of them survived the pounding waves, the rocky jetties, the universe of wildlife shrouded from sight under the water's surface. He could see why people treasured them, but he doubted very much whether they understood them. They just wanted some token, some artifact to take with them as a reminder of the experience. And for what? To sit and collect dust in some attic or garage somewhere? To be cracked and shattered inside a suitcase or grocery bag tossed into the trunk of a car? Maybe the lucky ones get displayed or decorated, but they are all eventually discarded.

His wife had not really cared for collecting shells. She would stop and admire them on the sand, but she never kept them. A native of the Carolina coast, she had explained to him once that a shell was beautiful because of what it was—a home. Some creature had formed the calcified armor as a way to survive, to protect itself from all the predators and caprices of life in the ocean. It was for this reason that she always left them as they lay. They belong to the beach, to the sand and sun and waves. To the place where their architects were born and had perished.

A giant, pregnant cloud rolled parallel to the beach a few miles out. Its shadow swept over the old man and cooled him for a few minutes. Saturdays were usually quiet. Most of the rental properties on the island began and ended their weeks on Saturdays, so the turnover usually meant the beaches were somewhat empty in the middle of the day. Only a few families were out this morning, which made for easier hunting. After examining a lovely moon snail specimen at his feet, the old man flipped it over with his stick to see if it was damaged at all. He found it to be perfectly whole, not even a crack. With a smile, he lifted the stick a few inches, then drove the end of it downward onto the shell.

A little girl of about seven standing nearby gasped when she saw what he had done. She asked in shock and amazement why he would break something so pretty.

"Because this is what the beach is made of. The shells have to stay here so the beach doesn't wash away."

"But we like those kind." Her voice wavered. "I wanted to give it to Mommy."

"Oh, I'm sure she'll find some more."

She took a step back from him, not taking her eye off the brown and white fragments he had scattered. A single tear hit the sand. He watched as she ran back to her parents and plopped down between them with her head squeezed between her

Shells

knees. In one comically precise synchronous movement, Mommy and Daddy both swiveled their heads to look at the old man. He shrugged and turned back toward his familiar path down the strand. After a few steps, he toed a rather large scallop shell, dislodging it from the wet sand just beyond the foaming surf. It was whole but had a hairline fracture that lightninged across its ridged outer surface. Again he lifted the stick and plunged it through the shell. And on he walked.

As the waves crashed and swirled farther and farther out, he made his way back along toward the staircase, toward his home. Occasionally, he'd find shells that he and the other scavengers had missed. These were destroyed in the same fashion as all the rest. As he neared his point of origin, the little girl who had interrupted his earlier holocaust caught his eye. Her parents frowned at him nearby. For a moment, he thought she would burst into tears again—it was hard to tell as she squinted in the sunlight. Instead, she marched over to the blanket spread out in front of their beach chairs. She picked up a plastic bucket and carried it bouncing against her sun-ripened leg, over to the old man. Her parents continued frowning, but now in puzzlement rather than disapproval. Before they realized her intent, the girl upended the bucket, spilling its contents onto the sand. An impressive assortment of shells and sand dollars tumbled out. She looked up at him with her head half-cocked.

"Don't you want to smash them?" she asked.

"Oh, I don't think Mommy and Daddy would be very happy about that."

Her mouth twisted in that childish expression of deep contemplation. After a beat, she stuck out her hand, clearly indicating a silent request for his stick. He hesitated, knowing what was about to happen. Nevertheless, with her pink hand remained outstretched in the same steadfast gesture, he complied, and now her parents could read the foreshadowed fate of their bounty. Within earshot of their protests, but beyond their physical reach, the girl's fist closed righteously around the stick and smashed it downward repeatedly in a rather fierce butter-churning motion. By the time they reached her and snatched away the weapon, every shell had been pulverized.

"What are you doing?" Mommy demanded.

"I'm saving the beach!"

The girl's simple, cryptic reply did nothing to assuage their anger, and the old man tried in vain to stifle his amusement.

"What is your problem?" Daddy demanded. This time, the question was posed to the old man.

Having faced similar confrontations before, he

knew better than to reason with them. After many years of being a father and a grandfather, he knew that children were quicker to understand because they had not yet been hardened by the emotional and intellectual undulations of experience. Unlike adults, children were not pursued by the demons of regret and shame. They were all future and no past.

"No problem here. I just want to go home and put my feet up. I'm not the same as I used to be, all young and full of energy like this one." He gestured to the girl, who spun around to chase a chain of low-flying pelicans. He reached out and gently took his stick back from the still fuming young father.

"But why did you let her destroy all our shells?"

"*Your* shells? Hm," he grunted.

"What? What does that mean?"

The weary old man sighed and clumped up the wooden stairs to cross the boardwalk back over the dunes. He heard the girl's father swear under his breath. At the top, where the wind gusted around him, he paused for a moment to watch the frustrated couple gather up their belongings. They folded the chairs and flipped sand out of the blanket. They gathered the girl's toys into a bucket and collapsed their umbrella. Meanwhile, the girl was hunched over the edge of a tidal pool. A thrill illuminated her face as she reached in and pulled

RIPPLES

out a bright orange starfish. She turned to share her discovery, but her parents were still busy, angrily loading all of their beach accoutrements into a canvas wagon with giant off-road tires. The light in her face dimmed.

She lowered the starfish back into the shallow pool and watched it sink beneath the gently rippling water. Turning around, she saw the old man at the top of the steps. She smiled and threw a surreptitious wave at him, then fell in step behind Mommy and Daddy as they sulked away. He answered her gesture with a conspiratorial nod before turning and shuffling along the boardwalk back to his house.

ACKNOWLEDGMENTS

Thank you to my family and friends for loving and supporting me through everything.

Thank you to my ENGL 1102 students for reading these stories (or at least pretending they did.)

Thank you to Ben Morrison for helping with the new cover design.

Thank you to Caitlin McDaniel, a friend and colleague whose support and feedback were instrumental in writing this collection.

Made in the USA
Middletown, DE
23 February 2024